THE
LITTLE PRINCE

ANTOINE DE SAINT-EXUPÉRY

ISBN: 978-93-61919-17-6

© Publishers

Publisher: Swan Books

Address: 4760-61, 23, Ansari Road,
Daryaganj, New Delhi-110002
Phone: 7011309851
WhatsApp: +91 7011309851
E-mail: swanbooks@yahoo.com

Edition: 2025

THE LITTLE PRINCE
ANTOINE DE SAINT-EXUPÉRY

CONTENTS

To LÉON WERTH

I apologise to children for dedicating this book to a grown-up. But I have a good excuse: this grown-up is the best friend I have ever had. I have another excuse too: this grown-up understands everything, even books for children. And I have a third excuse: this grown-up lives in France where he is hungry and cold and needs comforting. If these reasons are not enough, I should like to dedicate this book to the child this grown-up once was. All grown-ups were children once (but most of them have forgotten). So I will alter my dedication:

1

When I was six years old, I saw a magnificent picture in a book about the jungle called True Stories. It showed a boa constrictor swallowing a wild animal. This is what it looked like.

In the book it said: 'Boa constrictors swallow their prey whole, without chewing it. Afterwards they are unable to move. Then they sleep for six months while they digest.'

That set me thinking about all the things that go on in the jungle and, with a crayon, I did my first drawing. I called it drawing number one. It looked like this:

I showed my masterpiece to the grown-ups and asked if they found it scary.

They answered: 'What's scary about a hat?'

But my drawing was not of a hat. It was a boa constrictor digesting an elephant. So then I drew the inside of the boa, to help the grown-ups understand. They always need explanations. This is what my drawing number two looked like:

The grown-ups told me to forget about drawing elephants inside boa constrictors and to concentrate instead on geography, history, arithmetic and grammar. Which is why, at the age of six, seeing as my drawing number one and my drawing number two had been such a disaster, I gave up on a glorious career as an artist. Grown-ups never understand anything on their own, and it's nuisance for children to have to keep explaining things over and over again.

So I had to choose another profession, and I learned to be a pilot. I flew all around the world. And it is true that geography came in very handy. I could tell the difference between China and Arizona at a glance. Which is very useful, if you lose your way at night.

Over the past years, I have met lots of sensible people and spent a lot of time living in the world of grown-ups. I have seen them at close quarters, which has done nothing to change my opinion of them.

Whenever I met a grown-up who seemed fairly intelligent, I would test him with my drawing number one which I have always kept, to find out if he really was perceptive. But he would always reply: 'It's a hat.' So instead of talking to him about boa constrictors or the jungle or the stars, I'd come down to his level and discuss bridge, golf, politics and neckties. And the grown-up would be delighted to meet such a reasonable man.

2

And so I lived alone, with no one I could really talk to, until six years ago when my plane broke down in Sahara Desert. As I did not have a mechanic with me, or any passengers, I was going to have to make a complicated engine repair on my own. My life depended on it, since I had barely enough drinking water to last for only 8 days.

The first night, I lay down on the ground and fell asleep, miles and miles from any living soul. I was more cut off than a castaway adrift in the middle of the ocean. So you can imagine my astonishment when I was awakened at daybreak by a funny little voice saying: "Please, will you draw me a little lamb?"

"What"

"Draw me a little lamb…"

I leaped to my feet as if I had been struck by lightning. I rubbed my eyes and stared. And I saw the most extraordinary little fellow studying me intently. This is the best picture I have managed to draw of him from memory.

But of course my drawing is not nearly as delightful as the original. That is not my fault; the grown-ups had put a stop to my artistic career when I was six and I had never drawn anything other than my two boa constrictors.

I gazed at him in amazement. I was miles and miles from any living soul, remember. But my little fellow did not look lost. Nor did he seem weak with exhaustion, or hunger, or thirst, or fright. In no way did he look like a child lost in the middle of the desert miles and miles from any living soul. When at last I found my voice, I said to him: "What on earth are you doing here?"

And he repeated, very quietly, as if it were a matter of the utmost seriousness: "Please, will you draw me a little lamb?"

Here I was, miles and miles from any living soul and with my life in danger, but I was so baffled that I meekly prepared to do as he asked and took a pen and paper out of my pocket. And then I remembered that I had mostly studied geography, history, arithmetic and grammar, and I told the little fellow (somewhat irritably) that I couldn't draw. And he replied: "It doesn't matter. Draw me a little lamb."

As I had never done a picture of a lamb, I presented him with one of the only two drawings I could do: a boa constrictor from the outside. And I was astounded to hear the little fellow say: "No! No! I don't want an elephant inside a boa. A boa's too dangerous, and an elephant takes up too much room. My place is tiny. I need a lamb. Draw me a little lamb."

So I drew.

He scrutinised my effort and said: "No! That one looks very sickly. Draw another one."

I drew:

My little friend smiled indulgently: "Can't you see... that's not my lamb, it's a ram. It's got horns."

So I started all over again.

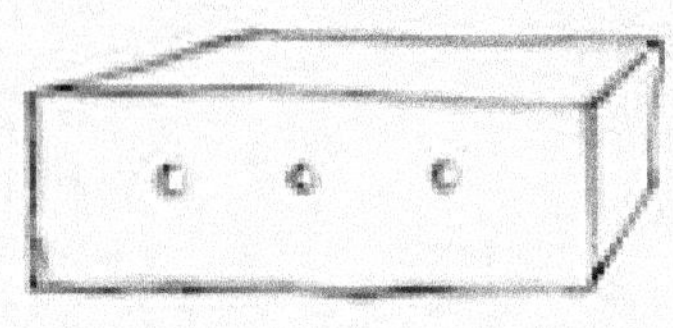

But again, he turned it down: "That one's too old. I want a lamb that will live for a long time."

I was in a hurry to start stripping down the engine and my patience was wearing thin, so I hastily sketched this:

And I said: "That's the crate. The lamb you want is inside."

And I was amazed to see my young critic's face light up: "That's exactly what I wanted! Do you think this lamb will need a lot of grass?"

"Why?"

"Because my place is tiny."

"I'm sure there'll be enough. I've given you a very little lamb."

He looked more closely at the drawing: "Not that little... Oh look! He's fallen asleep."

And that is how I made the acquaintance of the little prince.

3

It took me ages to work out where the little prince came from. He asked me lots of questions but never seemed to hear mine. I gradually pieced his story together from odd things he said. For instance, when he first caught sight of my plane (I shall not draw my airplane, that would be much too complicated for me), he asked me: "What's that thing?"

"It's not a thing. It flies. It's a plane. It's my plane."

And I was proud to tell him that I was a pilot and I flew planes.

Then he exclaimed: "What! You feel out of the sky!" "Yes", I replied modestly.

"Oh! That's funny."

And the little prince gave a tinkling laugh which I found extremely annoying. I expect people to take my troubles seriously.

Then he added: "So you came out of the sky too! What planet are you from?"

It suddenly dawned on me that he was giving me an important clue as to his mysterious appearance, and I said: "You're from another planet, aren't you?"

But he did not reply. Still staring at my plane, he gently nodded his head: "Of course, you can't have come from very far away in that thing."

And he stood lost in thought for a while. Then, taking my lamb out of his pocket, he examined his treasure.

You can imagine how intrigued I was by his allusion to other planets.

So I tried to find out more: "Where do you come from, little man? Where is 'your place'? Where do you want to take my lamb?"

He pondered for a while and replied: "The good thing about the crate is that at night it can be his house."

"Exactly. And if you behave, I'll give you a rope to tie him up during the day. And a stake."

The little prince was shocked: "Tie him up? What a strange thing to do!"

"But if you don't tie him up, he'll wander all over the place and get lost."

And my little friend burst out laughing again: "But where would he go?"

"Anywhere. Straight ahead of him."

Then the little prince remarked solemnly: "It wouldn't matter, my place is so tiny!"

And he added wistfully: "Straight ahead of him, nobody can go very far."

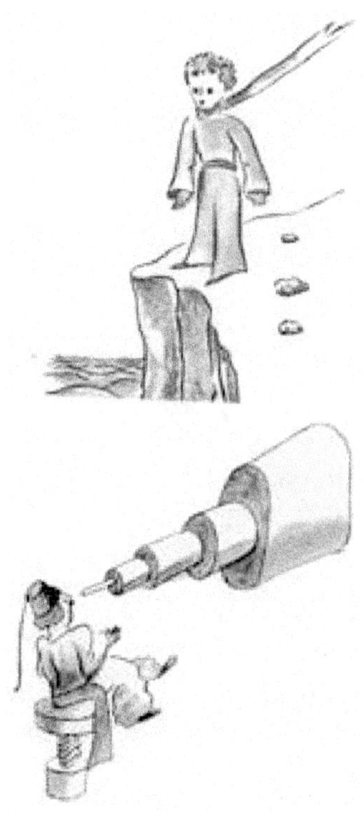

4

I had thus learned a second fact of great importance: this was that the planet the little prince came from was scarcely any larger than a house!

But that did not really surprise me much. I knew very well that in addition to the great planets -such as the Earth, Jupiter, Mars, Venus- to which we have given names, there are also hundreds of others, some of which are so small that one has a hard time seeing them through the telescope. When an astronomer discovers one of these he does not give it a name, but only a number. He might call it, for example, "Asteroid 325."

I have serious reason to believe that the planet from which the little prince came is the asteroid known as ? 612.

This asteroid has only once been seen through the telescope. That was by a Turkish astronomer, in 1909.

On making his discovery, the astronomer had presented it to the International Astronomical Congress, in a great demonstration. But he was in Turkish costume, and so nobody would believe what he said. Grown-ups are like that...

Fortunately, however, for the reputation of Asteroid B 612, a Turkish dictator made a law that his subjects, under pain of death, should change to European costume. So in 1920 the astronomer gave his demonstration all over again, dressed with impressive style and elegance. And this time everybody accepted his report.

If I have told you these details about the asteroid, and made a note of its number for you, it is on no account of the grown-ups and their ways. Grown-ups love figures. When you tell them that you have made a new friend, they never ask you any questions about essential matters. They never say to you, "What does his voice sound like? What games does he love best? Does he collect butterflies?" Instead, they demand: "How old is he? How many brothers has he? How much does he weigh? How much money does his father make?" Only from these figures do they think they have learned anything about him.

If you were to say to the grown-ups: "I saw a beautiful house made of rosy brick, with geraniums in the windows and doves on the roof," they would not be able to get any idea of that house at all. You would have to say to them: "I saw a house that cost 100.000 francs." Then they would exclaim: "Oh, what a pretty house that is!"

Just so, you might say to them: "The proof that the little prince existed is that he was charming, that he laughed, and that he was looking for a sheep. If anybody wants a sheep, that is a proof that he exists." And what good would it do tell them that? They would shrug their shoulders, and treat you like a child. But if you said to them: "The planet he came from is Asteroid B 612," then they would be convinced, and leave you in peace from their questions.

They are like that. One must not hold it against them. Children should always show great forbearance toward grown-up people.

But certainly, for us who understand life, figures are a matter of indifference. I should have liked to begin this story in the fashion of the fairy-tales. I should have liked to say: "Once upon a time there was a little prince who lived on a planet that was scarcely any bigger than himself, and who had need of a friend..."

To those who understand life, that would have given a much greater air of truth to my story.

I do not want any one to read my book carelessly. I have suffered too much grief in setting down these memories. Six years have already passed since my friend went away from me, with his sheep. If I try to describe him here, it is to make sure that I shall not forget him. To forget a friend is sad. Not every one has had a friend. And if I forget him, I may become like the grown-ups who are no longer interested in anything but figures...

It is for that purpose, again, that I have bought a box of paints and some pencils. It is hard to take up drawing again at my age, when I have never made any pictures except those of the boa constrictor from the outside and the boa constrictor from the inside, since I was six. I shall certainly try to make my portraits as true to life as possible. But I am not at all sure of success. One drawing goes along all right, and another has no resemblance to its subject. I make some errors, too, in the little prince's height: in one place he is too tall and in another too short. And I feel some doubts about the colour of his costume. So I fumble along as best I can, now good, now bad, and I hope generally fair- to-middling.

In certain more important details I shall make mistakes, also. But that is something that will not be my fault. My friend never explained anything to me. He thought, perhaps, that I was like himself. But I, alas, do not know how to see sheep through the walls of boxes. Perhaps I am a little like the grown-ups. I have had to grow old.

5

As each day passed I would learn, in our talk, something about the little prince's planet, his departure from it, his journey. The information would come very slowly, as it might chance to fall from his thoughts. It was in this way that I heard, on the third day, about the catastrophe of the baobabs.

This time, once more, I had the sheep to thank for it. For the little prince asked me abruptly –as if seized by a grave doubt- "It is true, isn't it, that sheep eat little bushes?"

"Yes, that is true." "Ah! I am glad!"

I did not understand why it was so important that sheep should eat little bushes. But the little prince added:

"Then it follows that they also eat baobabs?"

I pointed out to the little prince that baobabs were not little bushes, but, on the contrary, trees as big as castles; and that even if he took a whole herd of elephants away with him, the herd would not eat up one single baobab.

The idea of the herd of elephants made the little prince laugh.

　　　　　　　　　　　　　　　　　　THE LITTLE PRINCE

"We would have to put them one on top of the other," he said.

But he made a wise comment:

"Before they grow so big, the baobabs start out by being little."

"That is strictly correct," I said. "But why do you want the sheep to eat the little baobabs?"

He answered me at once, "Oh, come, come!", as if he were speaking of something that was self-evident. And I was obliged to make a great mental effort to solve this problem, without any assistance.

Indeed, as I learned, there were on the planet where the little prince lived —as on all planets- good plants and bad plants. In consequence, there were good seeds from good plants, and bad seeds from bad plants. But seeds are invisible. They sleep deep in the heart of the earth's darkness, until some one among them is seized with the desire to awaken. Then this little seed will stretch itself and begin —timidly at first- to push a charming little sprig inoffensively upward toward the sun. If it is only a sprout of radish or the sprig of a rose-bush, one would let it grow wherever it might wish. But when it is a bad plant, one must destroy it as soon as possible, the very first instant that one recognizes it.

Now there were some terrible seeds on the planet that was the home of the little prince; and these were the seeds of the baobab. The soil of that planet was infested with them. A baobab is something you will never, never be able to get rid of if you attend to it too late. It spreads over the entire planet. It bores clear through it with its roots. And if the planet is too small, and the baobabs are too many, they split it in pieces...

"It is a question of discipline," the little prince said to me later on. "When you've finished your own toilet in the morning, then it is time to attend to the toilet of your planet, just so, with the greatest care. You must see to it that you pull up regularly all the baobabs, at the very first moment when they can be distinguished from the rose- bushes which they resemble so closely in their earliest youth. It is very tedious work," the little prince added, "but very easy."

And one day he said to me: "You ought to make a beautiful drawing, so that the children where you live can see exactly how all this is. That would be very useful to them if they were to travel some day. Sometimes there is no harm in putting off a piece of work until another day. But when it is a matter of baobabs, that always means a catastrophe. I knew a planet that was inhabited by a lazy man. He neglected three little bushes..."

So, as the little prince described it to me, I have made a drawing of that planet. I do not much like to take the tone of a moralist. But the danger of the baobabs is so little understood, and such considerable risks would be run by anyone who might get lost on an asteroid, that for once I am breaking through my reserve. "Children," I say plainly, "watch out for the baobabs!"

My friends, like myself, have been skirting this danger for a long time, without ever knowing it; and so it is for them that I have worked so hard over this drawing. The lesson which I pass on by this means it worth all the trouble it has cost me.

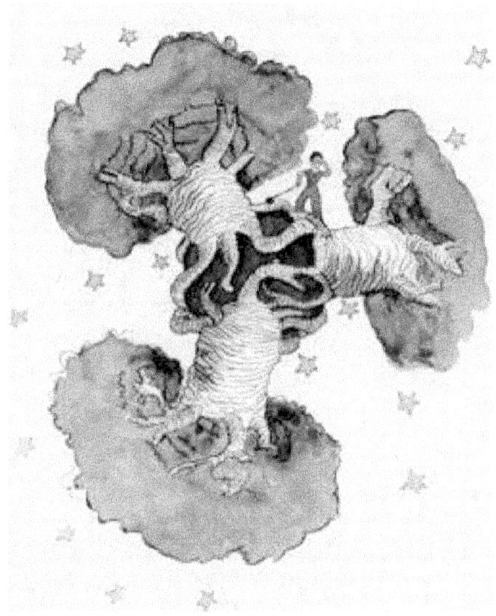

Perhaps you will ask me, "Why there are no other drawings in this book as magnificent and impressive as this drawing of the baobabs?"

The reply is simple. I have tried. But with the others I have not been successful. When I made the drawing of the baobabs I was carried beyond myself by the inspiring force of urgent necessity.

6

Oh, little prince! Bit by bit I came to understand the secrets of your sad little life... For a long time you had found your only entertainment in the quiet pleasure of looking at the sunset. I learned that new detail on the morning of the fourth day, when you said to me:

"I am very fond of sunsets. Come, let us go look at a sunset now."

"But he must wait," I said. "Wait? For what?"

"For the sunset. We must wait until it is time."

At first you seemed to be very much surprised. And then you laughed to yourself. You said to me:

"I am always thinking that I am at home!"

Just so. Everybody knows that when it is noon in the United States of America the sun is setting over France. If you could fly to France in one minute, you could go straight into the sunset, right from noon. Unfortunately, France is too far away for that. But on your tiny planet, my little prince, all you need do is move your chair a few steps. You can see the day end and the twilight falling whenever you like…

"One day," you said to me, "I saw the sunset forty-four times!"

And a little later you added:

"You know –one loves the sunset, when one is so sad…" "Were you so sad, then?" I asked, "on the day of the forty-four sunsets?"

But the little prince made no reply.

7

On the fifth day –again, as always, it was thanks to the sheep- the secret of the little prince's life was revealed to me. Abruptly, without anything to lead up to it, and as if the question had been born of long and silent meditation on his problem, he demanded:

"A sheep –if it eats little bushes, does it eat flowers, too?" A sheep," I answered, "eats anything it finds in its reach."

"Even flowers that have thorns?" "Yes, even flowers that have thorns." "Then the thorns –what use are they?"

I did not know. At that moment I was very busy trying to unscrew a bolt that had got stuck in my engine. I was very much worried, for it was becoming clear to me that the breakdown of my plane was extremely serious. And I had so little drinking water lest that I had to fear the worst.

"The thorns – what use are they?"

The little prince never let go of a question, once he had asked it. As for me, I was upset over that bolt. And I answered with the first thing that came into my head:

                                              THE LITTLE PRINCE

"The thorns are of no use at all. Flowers have thorns just for spite!"

"Oh!"

There was a moment of complete silence. Then the little prince flashed back at me, with a kind of resentfulness:

"I don't believe you! Flowers are weak creatures. They are naïve. They reassure themselves as best they can. They believe that their thorns are terrible weapons..."

I did not answer. At that instant I was saying to myself: "If this bolt still won't turn, I am going to knock it out with the hammer." Again the little prince disturbed my thoughts:

"And you actually believe that the flowers -"

"Oh, no!" I cried. "No, no, no! I don't believe anything. I answered you with the first thing that came into my head. Don't you see – I am very busy with matters of consequence!"

He stared at me, thunderstruck. "Matters of consequence!"

He looked at me there, with my hammer in my hand, my fingers black with engine-grease, bending down over an object which seemed to him extremely ugly...

"You talk just like the grown-ups!"

That made me a little ashamed. But he went on, relentlessly:

"You mix everything up together... You confuse everything..."

He was really very angry. He tossed his golden curls in the breeze.

"I know a planet where there is a certain red-faced gentleman. He has never smelled a flower. He has never looked a star. He has never loved any one. He has never done anything in his life but add up figures. And all day he says over and over, just like you:

'I am busy with matters of consequence!' And that makes him swell up with pride. But he is not a man – he is a mushroom!"

"A what?"

"A mushroom!"

The little prince was now white with rage.

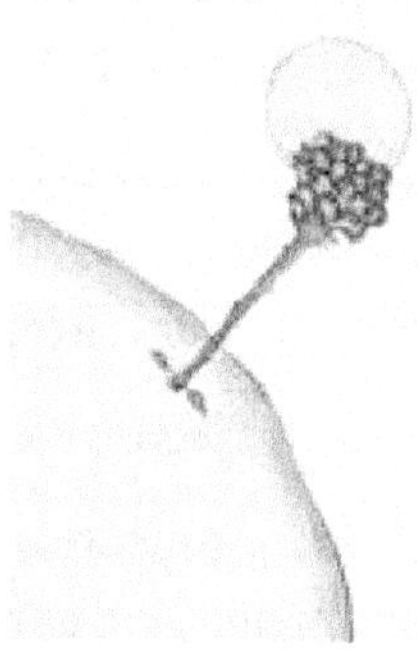

"The flowers have been growing thorns for millions of years. For millions of years the sheep have been eating them just the same. And it is not a matter of consequence to try to understand why the flowers go to so much trouble to grow thorns which are never of any use to them? Is the warfare between the sheep and the flowers not important? Is this not of more consequence than a fat red-faced gentleman's sums? And if I know – I, myself – one flower which is unique in the world, which grows nowhere but on my planet, but which one little sheep can destroy in a single bite some morning, without even noticing what he is doing – Oh! You think that is not important!"

His face turned from white to red as he continued:

"If some one loves a flower, of which just one single blossom grows in all the millions and millions of stars, it is enough to make him happy just to look at the stars. He can say to himself: 'Somewhere, my flower is there...' But if the sheep eats the flower, in one moment all his stars will be darkened... And you think that is not important!"

He could not say anything more. His words were choked by sobbing.

The night had fallen. I had let my tools drop from my hands. Of what moment now was my hammer, my bolt, or thirst, or death? On one star, one planet, my planet, the Earth, there was a little prince to be comforted. I took him in my arms, and rocked him. I said to him:

"The flower that you love is not in danger. I will draw you a muzzle for your sheep. I will draw you a railing to put around your flower. I will-"

I did not know what to say to him. I felt awkward and blundering. I did not know how I could reach him, where I could overtake him and go on hand in hand with him once more.

It is such a secret place, the land of tears

8

Isoon learned to know this flower better. On the little prince's planet the flowers had always been very simple. They had only one ring of petals; they took up no room at all; they were a trouble to nobody. One morning they would appear in the grass, and by night they would have faded peacefully away. But one day, from a seed blown from no one knew where, a new flower had come up; and the little prince had watched very closely over this small sprout which was not like any other small sprouts on his planet. It might, you see, have been a new kind of baobab.

But the shrub soon stopped growing, and began to get ready to produce a flower. The little prince, who was present at the first appearance of a huge bud, felt at once that some sort of miraculous apparition must emerge from it. But the flower was not satisfied to complete the preparations for her beauty in the shelter of her green chamber. She chose her colours with the greatest care. She dressed herself slowly. She adjusted her petals one by one. She did not wish to go out into the world all rumpled, like the field poppies. It was only in the full radiance of her beauty that she wished to appear. Oh, yes! She was a coquettish creature! And her mysterious adornment lasted for days and days.

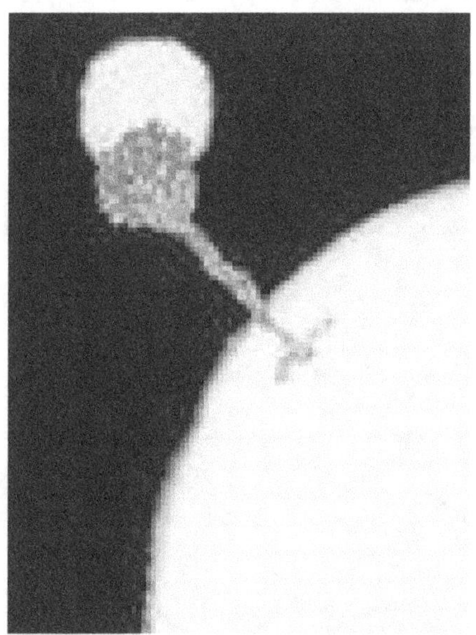

Then one morning, exactly at sunrise, she suddenly showed herself.

And, after working with all this painstaking precision, she yawned and said:

"Ah! I am scarcely awake. I beg that you will excuse me. My petals are still all disarranged…"

But the little prince could not restrain his admiration: "Oh! How beautiful you are!"

"Am I not?" the flower responded, sweetly. "And I was born at the same moment as the sun…"

The little prince could guess easily enough that she was not any too modest – but now moving – and exciting – she was!

"I think it is time for breakfast," she added an instant later. "If you would have the kindness to think of my needs-"

And the little prince, completely abashed, went to look for a sprinkling-can of fresh water. So, he tended the flower.

So, too, she began very quickly to torment him with her vanity – which was, if the truth be known, a little difficult to deal with. One day, for instance, when she was speaking of her four thorns, she said to the little prince:

"Let the tigers come with their clows!"

"There are no tigers on my planet," the little prince objected. "And, anyway, tigers do not eat weeds."

"I am not a weed," the flower replied, sweetly.

"Please excuse me…"

"I am not at all afraid of tigers," she went on, "but I have a horror of draughts. I suppose you wouldn't have a screen for me?"

"A horror of draughts – that is bad luck, for a plant," remarked the little prince, and added to himself, "This flower is a very complex creature…"

"At night I want you to put me under a glass globe. It is very cold where you live. In the place where I came from -"

But she interrupted herself at that point. She had come in the form of a seed. She could not have known anything of any other worlds. Embarrassed over having let herself be caught on the verge of such a naïve untruth, she coughed two or three times, in order to put the little prince in the wrong.

"The screen?"

"I was just going to look for it when you spoke to me..." Then she forced her cough a little more so that he should suffer from remorse just the same.

So the little prince, in spite of all the good will that was inseparable from his love, had soon come to doubt her. He had taken seriously words which were without importance, and it made him very unhappy.

"I ought not to have listened to her," he confided to me one day. "One never ought to listen to the flowers. One should simply look at them and breathe their fragrance. Mine perfumed all my planet. But I did not know how to take pleasure in all her grace. This tale of claws, which disturbed my so much, should only have filled my heart with tenderness and pity."

And he continued his confidences:

"The fact is that I did not know how to understand anything! I ought to have judged by deeds and not by words. She cast her fragrance and her radiance over me. I ought never to have run away from her... I ought to have guessed all the affection that lay behind her poor little stratagems. Flowers are so inconsistent! But I was too young to know how to love her..."

9

Ibelieve that for his escape he took advantage of the migration of a flock of wild birds. On the morning of his departure he put his planet in perfect order. He carefully cleaned out his active volcanoes. He possessed two active volcanoes; and they were very convenient for heating his breakfast in the morning. He also had one volcano that was extinct. But, as he said, "One never knows!" So he cleaned out the extinct volcano, too. If they are well cleaned out, volcanoes burn slowly and steadily, without any eruptions. Volcanic eruptions are like fires in a chimney.

On our earth we are obviously much too small to clean out our volcanoes. That is why they bring no end of trouble upon us.

The little prince also pulled up, with a certain sense of dejection, that last little shoots of the baobabs. He believed that he would never want to return. But on this last morning all these familiar tasks seemed very precious to him. And when he watered the flower for the last time, and prepared to place her under the shelter of her glass globe, he realized that he was very close to tears.

"Goodbye," he said to the flower. But she made no answer.

"Goodbye," he said again.

The flower coughed. But it was not because she had a cold. "I have been silly," she said to him, at last. "I ask your

forgiveness. Try to be happy..."

He was surprised by this absence of reproaches. He stood there all bewildered, the glass globe held arrested in midair. He did not understand this quiet sweetness.

"Of course I love you," the flower said to him. "It is my fault that you have not known it all the while. That is of no importance. But you – you have been just a foolish as I. Try to be happy... Let the glass globe be. I don't want it any more."

"But the wind-"

"My cold is not so bad as all that... The cool night air will do me good. I am a flower."

"But the animals-"

"Well, I must endure the presence of two or three caterpillars if I wish to become acquainted with the butterflies. It seems that they are very beautiful. And if not the butterflies –and the caterpillars- who will call upon me? You will be far away... As for the large animals – I am not at all afraid of any of them. I have my claws."

And, naively, she showed her four thorns. Then she added:

"Don't linger like this. You have decided to go away. Now go!"

For she did not want him to see her crying. She was such a proud flower...

10

He found himself in the neighbourhood of the asteroids 325, 326, 327, 328, 329, and 330. He began, therefore, by visiting them, in order to add to his knowledge.

The first of them was inhabited by a king. Clad in royal purple and ermine, he was seated upon a throne which was at the same time both simple and majestic.

"Ah! Here is a subject," exclaimed the king, when he saw the little prince coming.

And the little prince asked himself:

"How could he recognize me when he had never seen me before?"

He did not know how the world is simplified for kings. To them, all people are subjects.

"Approach, so that I may see you better," said the king, who felt consumingly proud of being at last a king over somebody.

The little prince looked everywhere to find a place to sit down; but the entire planet was crammed and obstructed by the king's magnificent ermine robe. So he remained standing upright, and, since he was tired, he yawned.

"It is contrary to etiquette to yawn in the presence of a king," the monarch said to him. "I forbid you to do do."

"I can't help it. I can't stop myself," replied the little prince, thoroughly embarrassed. "I have come on a long journey, and I have had no sleep..."

"Ah, then," the king said. "I order you to yawn. It is years since I have seen anyone yawing. Yawns, to me, are objects of curiosity. Come, now! Yawn again! It is an order."

"That frightens me... I cannot, any more..." murmured the little prince, now completely abashed.

"Hum! Hum!" replied the king. "Then I – I order you sometimes to yawn and sometimes to-"

He spluttered a little, and seemed vexed.

For what the king fundamentally insisted upon was that his authority should be respected. He tolerated no disobedience. He was an absolute monarch. But, because he was a very good man, he made his orders reasonable.

"If I ordered a general to change himself into a sea bird, and if the general did not obey me, that would not be the fault of the general. It would be my fault."

"May I sit down?" came now a timid inquiry from the little prince.

"I order you to do so," the king answered him, and majestically gathered in a fold of his ermine mantle.

But the little prince was wondering... The planet was tiny. Over what could this king really rule?

"Sire," he said to him, "I beg that you will excuse my asking you a question-"

"I order you to ask me a question," the king hastened to assure him.

"Sire-over what do you rule?"

"Over everything," said the king, with magnificent simplicity.

"Over everything?"

The king made a gesture, which took in his planet, the other planets, and all the stars.

"Over all that?" asked the little prince.

"Over all that," the king answered.

For his rule was not only absolute: it was also universal.

"And the stars obey you?"

"Certainly they do," the king said. "They obey instantly. I do not permit insubordination."

Such power was a thing for the little prince to marvel at. If he had been master of such complete authority, he would have been able to watch the sunset, not forty-four times in one day, but seventy-two, or even a hundred, or even two hundred times, without ever having to move his chair. And because he felt a bit sad as he remembered his little planet which he had forsaken, he plucked up his courage to ask the king a favour:

"I should like to see a sunset... Do me that kindness... Order the sun to set..."

"If I ordered a general to fly from one flower to another like a butterfly, or to write a tragic drama, or to change himself into a sea bird, and if the general did not carry out the order that he had received, which one of us would be in the wrong?" the king demanded "The general, or myself?"

"You," said the prince firmly.

"Exactly. One must require from each other the duty which each one can perform," the king went on. "Accepted authority rests first of all on reason. If you ordered your people to go and throw themselves into the sea, they would rise up in revolution. I have the right to require obedience because my orders are reasonable."

"Then my sunset?" the little prince reminded him: for he never forgot a question once he had asked it.

"You shall have your sunset. I shall command it. But, according to my science of government, I shall wait until conditions are favourable."

"When will that be?" inquired the little prince.

"Hum! Hum!" replied the king; and before saying anything else he consulted a bulky almanac. "Hum! Hum! That will be about –about- that will be this evening about twenty minutes to eight. And you will see how well I am obeyed!"

The little prince yawned. He was regretting his lost sunset. And then, too, he was already beginning to be a little bored.

"I have nothing more to do here," he said to the king. "So I shall set out on my way again."

"Do not go," said the king, who was very proud of having a subject. "Do not go. I will make you a Minister!"

"Minister of what?" "Minister of –of Justice!"

"But there is nobody here to judge!"

"We do not know that," the king said to him. "I have not yet made a complete tour of my kingdom. I am very old. There is no room here for a carriage. And it tires me to walk."

"Oh, but I have looked already!" said the little prince, turning around to give one more glance to the other side of the planet.

On that side, as on this, there was nobody at all… "Then you shall judge yourself," the king answered. "That is the most difficult thing of all. It is much more difficult to judge oneself than to judge others. If you succeed in judging yourself rightly, then you are indeed a man of true wisdom."

"Yes," said the little prince, "but I can judge myself anywhere. I do not need to live on this planet."

"Hum! Hum!" said the king. "I have good reason to believe that somewhere on my planet there is an old rat. I hear him at night. You can judge this old rat. From time to time you will condemn him to death. Thus his life will depend on your justice. But you will pardon him on each occasion; for he must be treated thriftily. He is the only one we have."

"I," replied the little prince, "do not like to condemn anyone to death. And now I think I will go on my way."

"No," said the king.

But the little prince, having now completed his preparations for departure, had no wish to grieve the old monarch.

"If your Majesty wishes to be promptly obeyed," he said, "he should be able to give me a reasonable order. He should be able, for example, to order me to be gone by the end of one minute. It seems to me that conditions are favourable…"

As the king made no answer, the little prince hesitated a moment. Then, with a sigh, he took his leave.

"I make you my Ambassador," the king called out, hastily.

He had a magnificent air of authority.

"The grown-ups are very strange," the little prince said to himself, as he continued on his journey.

11

The second planet was inhabited by a conceited man.

"Ah! Ah! I am about to receive a visit from an admirer!" he exclaimed, from afar, when he first saw the little prince coming.

For, to conceited people, all the others are admirers.

"Good morning," said the little prince. "That is as hat you are wearing."

"It is a hat for salutes," the conceited man replied. "It is to raise in salute when people acclaim me. Unfortunately, nobody at all ever passes this way."

"Yes?" said the little prince, who did not understand what the conceited man was talking about.

"Clap your hands, one against the other," the conceited man now directed him.

The little prince clapped his hands. The conceited man raised his hat in a modest salute.

"This is more entertaining than the visit to the king," the little prince said to himself. And he began again to clap his hands, one against the other. The conceited man again raised his hat in salute.

After five minutes of this exercise the little prince grew tired of the game's monotony.

"And what should one do to make the hat come down?" he asked.

But the conceited man did not hear him. Conceited people never hear anything but praise.

"Do you really admire me very much?" he demanded of the little prince.

"What does than mean –'admire'?"

"To admire means that you regards me as the handsomest, the best-dressed, the richest, and the most intelligent man on this planet."

"But you are the only man on your planet!"

"Do me this kindness. Admire me just the same."

"I admire you," said the little prince, shrugging his shoulders slightly, "but what is there in that to interest you so much?"

And the little prince went away.

"The grown-ups are certainly very odd," he said to himself, as he continued on his journey.

12

The next planet was inhabited by a tippler. This was a very short visit, but it plunged the little prince into deep dejection.

"What are you doing there?" he said to the tippler, whom he found settled down in silence before a collection of empty bottles and also a collection of full bottles.

"I am drinking," replied the tippler, with a lugubrious air.

"Why are you drinking?" demanded the little prince.

"So that I may forget," replied the tippler.

"Forget what?" inquired the little prince, who already was sorry for him.

"Forget that I am ashamed," the tippler confessed, hanging his head.

"Ashamed of what?" insisted the little prince, who wanted to help him.

"Ashamed of drinking!" The tippler brought his speech to an end, and shut himself up in an impregnable silence.

And the little prince went away, puzzled.

"The grown-ups are certainly very, very, odd," he said to himself, as he continued on his journey.

13

The fourth planet belonged to a businessman. This man was so much occupied that he did not even raise his head at the little prince's arrival.

"Good morning," the little prince said to him. "Your cigarette has gone out."

"Three and two make five. Five and seven make twelve. Twelve and three make fifteen. Good morning. Fifteen and seven make twenty-two. Twenty-two and six make twenty-eight. I haven't time to light it again. Twenty-six and five make thirty-one. Phew! Then that makes five-hundred- and-one million, six-hundred-twenty-two thousand, seven- hundred-thirty-one."

"Five hundred million what?" asked the little prince.

"Eh? Are you still there? Five-hundred-and-one million– I can't stop... I have so much to do! I am concerned with matters of consequence. I don't amuse myself with balderdash. Two and five make seven..."

"Five-hundred-and-one million what?" repeated the little prince, who never in his life had let go of a question once he had asked it.

The businessman raised his head.

"During the fifty-four years that I have inhabited this planet, I have been disturbed only three times. The first time was twenty-two years ago, when some giddy goose fell from goodness knows where. He made the most frightful noise that resounded all over the place, and I made four mistakes in my addition. The second time, eleven years ago, I was disturbed by an attack of rheumatism. I don't get enough exercise. I have no time for loafing. The third time –well, this is it! I was saying, then, five-hundred-and- one millions-"

"Millions of what?"

The businessman suddenly realized that there was no hope of being left in peace until he answered this question.

"Millions of those little objects," he said, "which one sometimes sees in the sky."

"Flies?"

"Oh, no. Little glittering objects." "Bees?"

"Oh, no. Little objects that set lazy people to idle dreaming. As for me, I am concerned with matters of consequence. There is no time for idle dreaming in my life."

"Ah! You mean the stars?" "Yes, that's it. The stars."

"And what do you do with five-hundred millions of stars?"

"Five-hundred-and-one million, six-hundred-twenty- two thousand, seven-hundred-thirty-one. I am concerned with matters of consequence: I am accurate."

"And what do you do with these stars?"

"What do I do with them?"

"Yes."

"Nothing. I own them."

"You own the stars?" "Yes."

"But I have already seen a king who-"

"Kings do not own, they reign over. It is a very different matter."

"And what good does it do you to own the stars?"

"It does me the good of making me rich."

"And what good does it do you to be rich?"

"It makes it possible for me to buy more stars, if any are discovered."

"This man," the little prince said to himself, "reasons like my poor tippler..."

Nevertheless, he still had some more questions.

"How is it possible for one to own the stars?"

"To whom do they belong?" the businessman retorted, peevishly.

"I don't know. To nobody."

"Then they belong to me, because I was the first person to think of it."

"Is that all that is necessary?"

"Certainly. When you find a diamond that belongs to nobody, it is yours. When you discover an island that belongs to nobody, it is yours. When you get an idea before any one else, you take out a patent on it: it is yours. So with me: I own the stars, because nobody else before me ever thought of owning them."

"Yes, that is true," said the little prince. "And what do you do with them?"

"I administer them," replied the businessman. "I count them and recount them. It is difficult. But I am a man who is naturally interested in matters of consequence."

The little prince was still not satisfied.

"If I owned a silk scarf," he said, "I could put it around my neck and take it away with me. If I owned a flower, I could pluck that flower and take it away with me. But you cannot pluck the stars from heaven..."

"No. But I can put them in the bank." "Whatever does that mean?"

"That means that I write the number of my stars on a little paper. And then I put this paper in a drawer and lock it with a key."

"And that is all?"

"That is enough," said the businessman.

"It is entertaining," thought the little prince. "It is rather poetic. But it is of no great consequence."

On matters of consequence, the little prince had ideas which were very different from those of the grown-ups.

"I myself own a flower," he continued his conversation with the businessman, "which I water every day. I own three volcanoes, which I clean out every week (for I also clean out the one that is extinct; one never knows).

It is of some use to my volcanoes, and it is of some use to my flower, that I own them. But you are of no use to the stars..."

The businessman opened his mouth, but he found nothing to say in answer. And the little prince went away.

"The grown-ups are certainly altogether extraordinary," he said simply, talking to himself as he continued on his journey.

14

The fifth planet was very strange. It was the smallest of all. There was just enough room on it for a street

lamp and a lamplighter. The little prince was not able to reach any explanation of the use of a street lamp and a lamplighter, somewhere in the heavens, on a planet which was so small that it had no people, and not one house. But he said to himself, nevertheless:

"It may well be that this man is absurd. But he is not so absurd as the king, the conceited man, the businessman, and the tippler. For at least his work has some meaning. When he lights his street lamp, it is as if he brought one more star to life, or one flower. When he puts out his lamp, he sends the flower, or the star, to sleep. That is a beautiful occupation. And since it is beautiful, it is truly useful."

When he arrived on the planet he respectfully saluted the lamplighter.

"Good morning, sir. Why have you just put out your lamp?"

"Those are the orders," replied the lamplighter. "Good morning."

"What are the orders?"

"The orders are that I put out my lamp. Good evening."

And he lighted his lamp again.

"But why have you just lighted it again?"

"Those are the others," replied the lamplighter. "I do not understand," said the little prince.

"There is nothing to understand," said the lamplighter. "Orders are orders. Good morning."

And he put out his lamp.

Then he mopped his forehead with a handkerchief decorated with red squares.

"I follow a terrible profession. In the old days it was reasonable. I put the lamp out in the morning, and in the evening I lighted it again. I had the rest of the day for relaxation and the rest of the night for sleep."

"And the orders have been changed since that time?"

"The orders have not been changed," said the lamplighter. "That is the tragedy! From year to year the planet has turned more rapidly and the orders have not been changed!"

"Then what?" asked the little prince.

"Then –the planet now makes a complete turn every minute, and I no longer have a single second for repose. Once every minute I have to light my lamp and put it out!"

"That is very funny! A day lasts only one minute, here where you live!"

"It is not funny at all!" said the lamplighter. "While we have been talking together a month has gone by."

"A month?"

"Yes, a month. Thirty minutes. Thirty days. Good evening."

And he lighted his lamp again.

As the little prince watched him, he felt that he loved this lamplighter who was so faithful to his orders. He remembered the sunsets which he himself had gone to seek, in other days, merely by pulling up his chair; and he wanted to help his friend.

"You know," he said, "I can tell you a way you can rest whenever you want to…"

"I always want to rest," said the lamplighter.

For it is possible for a man to be faithful and lazy at the same time.

The little prince went on with his explanation:

"Your planet is so small that three strides will take you all the way around it. To be always in the sunshine, you need only walk along rather slowly. When you want to rest, you will walk –and the day will last as long as you like."

"That doesn't do me much good," said the lamplighter. "The one thing I love in life is to sleep."

"Then you're unlucky," said the little prince.

"I am unlucky," said the lamplighter. "Good morning." And he put out his lamp.

"That man," said the little prince to himself, as he continued farther on his journey, "that man would be scorned by all the others: by the king, by the conceited man, by the tippler, by the businessman. Nevertheless he is the only one of them all who does not seem to me ridiculous. Perhaps that is because he is thinking of something else besides himself."

He breathed a sigh of regret, and said to himself again: "Than man is the only one of them all whom I could have made my friend. But his planet is indeed too small. There is no room on it for two people..."

What the little prince did not dare confess was that he was sorry most of all to leave this planet, because it was blest every day with one thousand four hundred and forty sunsets in twenty-four hours!

15

The sixth planet was ten times larger than the last one. It was inhabited by an old gentleman who wrote voluminous books.

"Oh, look! Here is an explorer!" he exclaimed to himself when he saw the little prince coming.

The little prince sat down on the table and panted a little. He had already travelled so much and so far!

"Where do you come from?" the old gentleman said to him.

"What is that big book?" said the little prince. "What are you doing?"

"I am a geographer," said the old gentleman.

"What is a geographer?" asked the little prince.

"A geographer is a scholar who knows the location of all the seas, rivers, towns, mountains, and deserts."

"That is very interesting," said the little prince. "Here at last is a man who has a real profession!" And he cast a look around him at the planet of geographer. It was the most magnificent and stately planet that he had ever seen.

"Your planet is very beautiful," he said. "Has it any oceans?"

"I couldn't tell you," said the geographer.

"Ah!" The little prince was disappointed. "Has it any mountains?"

"I couldn't tell you," said the geographer. "And towns, and rivers, and deserts?"

"I couldn't tell you that, either." "But you are a geographer!"

"Exactly," the geographer said

"But I am not an explorer. I haven't a single explorer on my planet. It is not the geographer who goes out to count the towns, the rivers, the mountains, the seas, the oceans, and the deserts. The geographer is much too important to go loafing about. He does not leave his desk. But he receives the explorers in his study. He asks them questions, and he notes down what they recall of their travels. And if the recollections of any one among them seem interesting to him, the geographer orders an inquiry into that explorer's moral character."

"Why is that?"

"Because an explorer who told lies would bring disaster on the books of the geographer. So would an explorer who drank too much."

"Why is that?" asked the little prince.

"Because intoxicated people see double. Then the geographer would note down two mountains in a place where there was only one."

"I know some one," said the little prince, "who would make a bad explorer."

"That is possible. Then, when the moral character of the explorer is shown to be good, an inquiry is ordered into his discovery."

"One goes to see it?"

"No that would be too complicated. But one requires the explorer to furnish proofs. For example, if the discovery in question is that of a large mountain, one requires that large stones be brought back from it."

The geographer was suddenly stirred to excitement. "But you-you come from far away! You are an explorer! You shall describe your planet to me!"

And, having opened his big register, the geographer sharpened his pencil. The recitals of explorers are put down first in pencil. One waits until the explorer has furnished proofs, before putting them down in ink.

"Well?" said the geographer expectantly.

"Oh, where I live," said the little prince, "it is not very interesting. It is all so small. I have three volcanoes. Two volcanoes are active and the other is extinct. But one never knows."

"One never knows," said the geographer.

"I have also a flower."

"We do not record flowers," said the geographer.

"Why is that? The flower is the most beautiful thing on my planet!"

"We do not record them," said the geographer, "because they are ephemeral."

"What does that mean –'ephemeral'?"

"Geographies," said the geographer, "are the books which, of all books, are most concerned with matters of consequence. They never become old-fashioned. It is very rarely that a mountain changes its position. It is very rarely that an ocean empties itself of its waters. We write of eternal things."

"But extinct volcanoes may come to life again," the little prince interrupted. "What does that mean- 'ephemeral'?"

"Whether volcanoes are extinct or alive, it comes to the same thing for us," said the geographer. "The thing that matters to us is the mountain. It does not change."

"But what does that mean-'ephemeral'?" repeated the little prince, who never in his life had let go of a question, once he had asked it.

"It means, 'which is in danger of speedy disappearance'." "Is my flower in danger of disappearance?"

"Certainly it is."

"My flower is ephemeral," the little prince said to himself, "and she has only four thorns to defend herself against the world. And I have left her on my planet, all alone!"

That was his first moment of regret. But he took courage once more.

"What place would you advise me to visit know?" he asked.

"The planet Earth," replied the geographer. "It has a good reputation.

And the little prince went away, thinking of his flower.

16

So then the seventh planet was Earth.

The Earth is not just an ordinary planet! One can count, there, one hundred and eleven kings (including, of course, the African kings), seven thousand geographers, nine hundred thousand businessmen, seven-and-a-half million drunkards, three-hundred-eleven million vain men; in other words, about two billion grown-ups.

To give you an idea of the size of the Earth, I will tell you that before the invention of electricity it was necessary to maintain, over the whole of the six continents, a veritable army of four-hundred-sixty-two thousand, five hundred and eleven lamplighters for the street lamps.

Seen from some distance, that would make a splendid effect. The movements of this army would be regulated like those of the ballet in the opera. First would come the turn of the lamplighters of New Zealand and Australia. Having set their lamps alight, these would go off to sleep. Next, the lamplighters of China and Siberia would enter for their steps in the dance, and then they

 THE LITTLE PRINCE

too would be waved back into the wings. After that would come
the turn of the lamplighters of Russia and the Indies; then those
of Africa and Europe; then those of South America; then those
of North America. And never would they make a mistake in the
order of their entry upon the stage. It would be magnificent.

Only the man who was in charge of the single lamp at the
North Pole, and his colleague who was responsible for the single
lamp at the South Pole-only these two would live free from toil
and care: they would be busy twice a year.

17

When one wishes to play the wit, he sometimes wanders a little from the truth. I have not been altogether honest in what I have told you about the lamplighters. And I realize that I run the risk of giving a false idea of our planet to those who do not know it. Men occupy a very small space upon the Earth. If the two billion inhabitants who people its surface were all to stand upright and somewhat crowded together, as they do for some big public assembly, they could easily be put into one public square twenty miles long and twenty miles wide. All humanity could be pilled up on a small Pacific islet.

The grown-ups, to be sure, will not believe you when you tell them that. They imagine that they fill a great deal of space. They fancy themselves as important as the baobabs. You should advise them, then, to make their own calculations. They adore figures, and that will please them. But do not waste your time on this extra task. It is unnecessary. You have, I know, confidence in me.

When the little prince arrived on the Earth, he was very much surprised not to see any people. He was beginning to be afraid he had come to the wrong planet, when a coil of gold, the colour of the moonlight, flashed across the sand.

"Good evening," said the little prince courteously.

"Good evening," said the snake.

"What planet is this on which I have come down?" asked the little prince.

"This is the Earth; this is Africa," the snake answered.

"Ah! Then there are no people on the Earth?"

"This is the desert. There are no people in the desert. The Earth is large," said the snake.

The little prince sat down on a stone, and raised his eyes toward the sky.

"I wonder," he said, "whether the stars are set alight in heaven so that one day each one of us may find his own again... Look at my planet. It is right there above us. But how far away it is!"

"It is beautiful," the snake said. "What has brought you here?"

"I have been having some trouble with a flower," said the little prince.

"Ah!" said the snake.

And they were both silent.

"Where are the people?" the little prince at last took up the conversation again. "It is a little lonely in the desert..."

"It is also lonely among people," the snake said. The little prince gazed at him for a long time.

"You are a funny animal," he said at last. "You are no thicker than a finger..."

"But I am more powerful than the finger of a king," said the snake.

The little prince smiled.

"You are not very powerful. You haven't even any feet. You cannot even travel..."

"I can carry you farther than any ship could take you," said the snake.

He twined himself around the little prince's ankle, like a golden bracelet.

"Whomever I touch, I send back to the earth from whence they came," the snake spoke again. "But you are innocent and true, and you come from a star..."

The little prince made no reply.

"You move me to pity-you are so weak on this Earth made of granite," the snake said. "I can help you, some day, if you grow too homesick for your own planet. I can-"

"Oh! I understand you very well," said the little prince. "But why do you always speak in riddles?"

"I solve them all," said the snake.

And they were both silent.

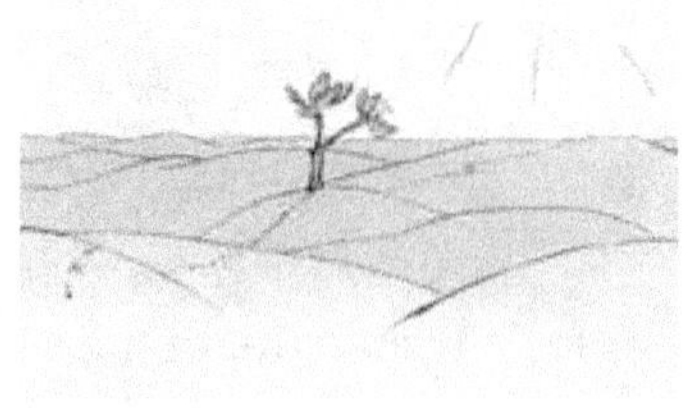

18

The little prince crossed the desert and met with only one flower. It was a flower with three petals, a flower of no account at all.

"Good morning," said the little prince.

"Good morning," said the flower.

"Where are the people?" the little prince asked, politely.

The flower had once seen a caravan passing.

"People?" she echoed. "I think there are six or seven of them in existence. I saw them, several years ago. But one never knows where to find them. The wind blows them away. They have no roots, and that makes their life very difficult."

"Goodbye," said the little prince.

"Goodbye," said the flower.

19

After that, the little prince climbed a high mountain. The only mountains he had ever known were the three volcanoes, which came up to his knees. And he used the extinct volcano as a foot-stool. "From a mountain as high as this one," he said to himself, "I shall be able to see the whole planet at one glance, and all the people..."

But he saw nothing, save peaks of rock that were sharpened like needles.

"Good morning," he said courteously.

"Good morning-Good morning-Good morning," answered the echo.

"Who are you?" said the little prince.

"Who are you-Who are you-Who are you?" answered the echo.

"Be my friends. I am all alone," he said.

"I am all alone-all alone-all alone," answered the echo.

"What a queer planet!" he thought. "It is altogether dry, and altogether pointed, and altogether harsh and forbidding. And the people have no imagination. They repeat whatever one says to them... On my planet I had a flower; she always was the first to speak..."

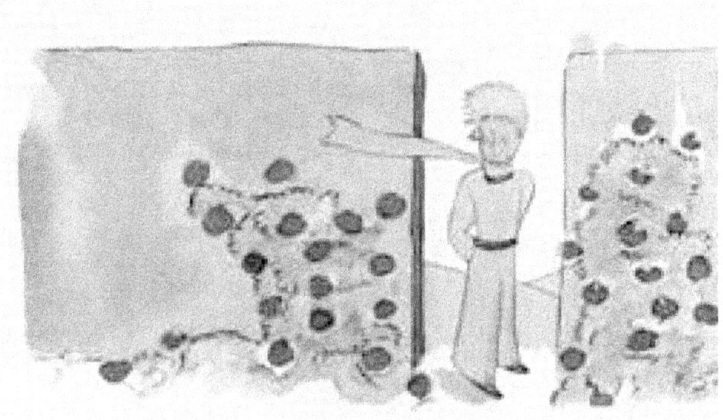

20

But it happened that after walking for a long time through sand, and rocks, and snow, the little prince at last came upon a road. And all roads lead to the abodes of people.

"Good morning," he said.

He was standing before a garden, all a-bloom with roses. "Good morning," said the roses.

The little prince gazed at them. They all looked like his flower.

"Who are you?" he demanded, thunderstruck.

"We are roses," the roses said.

And he was overcome with sadness. His flower had told him that she was the only one of her kind in all the universe. And here were five thousand of them, all alike, in one single garden!

"She would be very much annoyed," he said to himself, "if she could see that... She would cough most dreadfully, and she would pretend that she was dying, to avoid being laughed at. And I should be obliged to pretend that I was nursing her back to life-for if I did not do that, to humble myself also, she would really allow herself to die..."

Then he went on with his reflections: "I thought that I was rich, with a flower that was unique in all the world; and all I had was a common rose. A common rose, and three volcanoes that come up to my knees-and one of them perhaps extinct forever... That doesn't make me a very great prince..."

And he lay down in the grass and cried.

21

It was then that the fox appeared.

"Good morning," said the fox.

"Good morning," the little prince responded politely, although when he turned around he saw nothing.

"I am right here," the voice said, "under the apple tree."

"Who are you?" asked the little prince, and added, "You are very pretty to look at."

"I am a fox," the fox said.

"Come and play with me," proposed the little prince. "Iam so unhappy."

"I can't play with you," the fox said. "I am not tamed."

"Ah! Please excuse me," said the little prince.

But, after some thought, he added:

#x201C;What does that mean-'tame'?"

"You do not live here," said the fox. "What is it that you are looking for?"

"I am looking for people," said the little prince. "What does that mean-'tame'?"

"People," said the fox. "They have guns, and they hunt. It is very disturbing. They also raise chickens. These are their only interests. Are you looking for chickens?"

"No," said the little prince. "I am looking for friends. What does that mean-'tame'?"

"It is an act too often neglected," said the fox. "It means to establish ties."

"'To establish ties'?"

"Just that," said the fox. "To me, you are still nothing more than a little boy who is just like a hundred thousand other little boys. And I have no need of you. And you, on your part, have no need of me. To you, I am nothing more than a fox like a hundred thousand other foxes. But if you tame me, then we shall need each other. To me, you will be unique in all the world. To you, I shall be unique in all the world..."

"I am beginning to understand," said the little prince. "There is a flower... I think that she has tamed me..."

"It is possible," said the fox. "On the Earth one sees all sorts of things."

"Oh, but this is not on the Earth!" said the little prince. The fox seemed perplexed, and very curious.

"On another planet?" "Yes."

"Are there hunters on that planet?" "No."

"Ah, that is interesting! Are there chickens?" "No."

"Nothing is perfect," sighed the fox. But the fox came back to her idea.

"My life is very monotonous," she said. "I hunt chickens; people hunt me. All the chickens are just alike, and all people are just alike. And, in consequence, I am a little bored. But if you tame me, it will be as if the sun came to shine on my life. I shall know the sound of a step that will be different from all the others. Other steps send me hurrying back underneath the ground. Yours will call me, like music, out of my burrow. And then look: you see the grain-fields down yonder? I do not eat bread. Wheat is of no use to me. And that is sad. But you have hair that is the colour of gold. Think how wonderful that will be when you have tamed me! The grain, which is also golden, will bring me back the thought of you. And I shall love to listen to the wind in the wheat..."

The fox gazed at the little prince, for a long time. "Please-tame me!" she said.

"I want to, very much," the little prince replied. "But I have not much time. I have friends to discover, and a great many things to understand."

"One only understands the things that one tames," said the fox. "People have no more time to understand anything.

They buy things all ready made at the shops. But there is no shop anywhere where one can buy friendship, and so people have no friends any more. If you want a friend, tame me…"

"What must I do, to tame you?" asked the little prince. "You must be very patient," replied the fox. "First you will sit down at a little distance from me -like that- in the grass. I shall look at you out of the corner of my eye, and you will say nothing. Words are the source of misunderstandings. But you will sit a little closer to me, every day…"

The next day the little prince came back.

"It would have been better to come back at the same hour," said the fox. "If, for example, you came at four o'clock in the afternoon, then at three o'clock I shall begin to be happy. I shall feel happier and happier as the hour advances. At four o'clock, I shall already be worrying and jumping about. I shall show you how happy I am! But if you come at just any time, I shall never know at what hour my heart is to be ready to greet you… One must observe the proper rites…"

"What is a 'rite'?" asked the little prince.

"Those also are actions too often neglected," said the fox. "They are what make one day different from other days, one hour from other hours. There is a rite, for example, among my hunters. Every Thursday they dance with the village girls. So Thursday is a wonderful day for me! I can take a walk as far as the vineyards. But if the hunters danced at just any time, every day would be like every other day, and I should never have any vacation at all."

So the little prince tamed the fox. And when the hour of his departure drew near-

"Ah," said the fox, "I shall cry."

"It is your own fault," said the little prince. "I never wished you any sort of harm; but you wanted me to tame you..."

"Yes, that is so," said the fox.

"But now you going to cry!" said the little prince.

"Yes, that is so," said the fox.

"Then it has done you no good at all!"

"It has done me good," said the fox, "because of the colour of the wheat fields." And then she added:

"Go and look again at the roses. You will understand now that yours is unique in all the world. Then come back to say goodbye to me, and I will make you a present of a secret."

The little prince went away, to look again at the roses.

"You are not at all like my rose," he said. "As yet you are nothing. No one has tamed you, and you have tamed no one. You are like my fox when I first knew her. She was only a fox like a hundred other foxes. But I have made her my friend, and now she is unique in all the world."

And the roses were very much embarrassed.

"You are beautiful, but you are empty," he went on. "One could not die for you. To be sure, an ordinary passerby would think that my rose looked just like you- the rose that belongs to me. But in herself alone she is more important than all the hundreds of you other roses: because it is she that I have watered; because it is she that I have put under the glass globe; because it is she that I have sheltered behind the screen; because it is for her that I have killed the caterpillars (except the two or three that we saved to become butterflies); because it is she that I have listened to, when she grumbled, or boasted, or even sometimes when she said nothing. Because he is my rose."

And he went back to meet the fox. "Goodbye," he said.

"Goodbye," said the fox. "And now here is my secret, a very simple secret: It is only with the heart that one can see rightly; what is essential is invisible to the eye."

"What is essential is invisible to the eye," the little prince repeated, so that he would be sure to remember.

"It is the time you have wasted for your rose that makes your rose so important."

"It is the time I have wasted for my rose-" said the little prince, so that he would be sure to remember.

"People have forgotten this truth," said the fox. "But you must not forget it. You become responsible, forever, for what you have tamed. You are responsible for your rose..."

"I am responsible for my rose," the little prince repeated, so that he would be sure to remember.

22

"G ood morning," said the little prince.

"Good morning," said the railway switchman. "What do you do here?" the little prince asked.

"I sort out travellers, in bundles of a thousand," said the switchman. "I send off the trains that carry them: now to the right, now to the left."

And a brilliantly lighted express train shook the switchman's cabin as it rushed by with a roar like thunder.

"They are in a great hurry," said the little prince. "What are they looking for?"

"Not even the locomotive engineer knows that," said the switchman.

And a second brilliantly lighted express thundered by, in the opposite direction.

"Are they coming back already?" demanded the little prince.

"These are not the same ones," said the switchman. "It is an exchange."

"Were they not satisfied where they were?" asked the little prince.

"No one is ever satisfied where he is," said the switchman.

And they heard the roaring thunder of a third brilliantly lighted express.

"Are they pursuing the first travelers?" demanded the little prince.

"They are pursuing nothing at all," said the switchman. "They are asleep in there, or if they are not asleep they are yawning. Only the children are flattening their noses against the window-panes."

"Only the children know what they are looking for," said the little prince. "They waste their time over a rag doll and it becomes very important to them; and if anybody takes it away from them, they cry..."

"They are lucky," the switchman said.

23

"G ood morning," said the little prince.

"Good morning," said the merchant.

This was the merchant who sold pills that had been invented to quench thirst. You need only swallow one pill a week, and you would feel no need of anything to drink.

"Why are you selling those?" asked the little prince.

"Because they save a tremendous amount of time," said the merchant. "Computations have been made by experts. With these pills, you save fifty-three minutes in every week."

"And what do I do with those fifty-three minutes?"

"Anything you like..."

"As for me," said the little prince to himself, "if I had fifty-three minutes to spend as I liked, I should walk at my leisure toward a spring of fresh water."

24

It was now the eighth day since I had had my accident in the desert, and I had listened to the story of the merchant as I was drinking the last drop of my water supply.

"Ah," I said to the little prince, "these memories of yours are very charming; but I have not yet succeeded in repairing my plane; I have nothing more to drink; and I, too, should be very happy if I could walk at my leisure toward a spring of fresh water!"

"My friend the fox-" the little prince said to me.

"My dear little man, this is no longer a matter that has anything to do with the fox!"

"Why not?"

"Because I am about to die of thirst..."

He did not follow my reasoning, and he answered me: "It is a good thing to have a friend, even if one is about to die. I, for instance, am very glad to have a fox as a friend..."

"He has no way of guessing the danger," I said to myself. "He has never been either hungry or thirsty. A little sunshine is all that he needs..."

But he looked at me steadily, and replied to my thought:

"I am thirsty, too. Let us look for a well..."

I made a gesture of weariness. It is absurd to look for a well, at random, in the immensity of the desert. But nevertheless we started walking.

When we had trudged along for several hours, in silence, the darkness fell, and the stars began to come out. Thirst had made me a little feverish, and I looked at them as if I were in a dream. The little prince's last words came reeling back into my memory:

"Then you are thirsty, too?" I demanded.

But he did not reply to my question. He merely said to me:

"Water may also be good for the heart..."

I did not understand this answer, but I said nothing. I knew very well that is was impossible to cross-examine him.

He was tired. He sat down. I sat down beside him. And, after a little silence, he spoke again:

"The stars are beautiful, because a flower that cannot be seen."

I replied, "Yes, that is so." And, without saying anything more, I looked across the ridges of sand that were stretched out before us in the moonlight.

"The desert is beautiful," the little prince added.

And that was true. I have always loved the desert. One sits down on a desert sand dune, sees nothing, hears nothing. Yet through the silence something throbs, and gleams...

"What makes the desert beautiful," said the little prince, "is that somewhere it hides a well..."

I was astonished by a sudden understanding of that mysterious radiation of the sands. When I was a little boy I lived in an old house, and legend told us that a treasure was buried there. To be sure, no one had ever known how to find it; perhaps no one had ever even looked for it. But it cast an enchantment over that house. My home was hiding a secret in the depths of its heart...

"Yes," I said to the little prince. "The house, the stars, the desert- what gives them their beauty is something that is invisible!"

"I am glad," he said, "that you agree with my fox."

As the little prince dropped off the sleep, I took him in my arms and set out walking once more. I felt deeply moved, and stirred. It seemed to me that I was carrying a very fragile treasure. It seemed to me, even, that there was nothing more fragile on all the Earth. In the moonlight I looked at his pale forehead, his closed eyes, his locks of hair that trembled in the wind, and I said to myself: "What I see here is nothing but a shell. What is most important is invisible..."

As his lips opened slightly with the suspicion of a half- smile, I said to myself, again: "What moves me so deeply, about this little prince who is sleeping here, is his loyalty to a flower-the image of a rose that shines through his whole being like the flame of a lamp, even when he is asleep..." And I felt him to be more fragile still. I felt the need of protecting him, as if he himself were a flame that might be extinguished by a little puff of wind...

And, as I walked on so, I found the well, at daybreak.

25

People," said the little prince, "set out on their way in express trains, but they do not know what they are looking for. Then they rush about, and get excited, and turn round and round..."

And he added:

"It is not worth the trouble..."

The well that we had come to was not like the wells of the Sahara. The wells of the Sahara are mere holes dug in the sand. This one was like a well in a village. But there was no village here, and I thought I must be dreaming...

"It is strange," I said to the little prince. "Everything is ready for use: the pulley, the bucket, the rope..."

He laughed, touched the rope, and set the pulley to working. And the pulley moaned, like an old weathervane which the wind has long since forgotten.

"Do you hear?" said the little prince. "We have wakened the well, and it is singing..."

I did not want to tire himself with the rope.

Leave it to me," I said. "It is too heavy for you."

I hoisted the bucket slowly to the edge of the well and set it there-happy, tired as I was, over my achievement. The song of the pulley was still in my ears, and I could see the sunlight shimmer in the still trembling water.

"I am thirsty for this water," said the little prince. "Give me some of it to drink..."

And I understood what he had been looking for.

I raised the bucket to his lips. He drank, his eyes closed. It was as sweet as some special festival treat. This water was indeed a different thing from ordinary nourishment. Its sweetness was born of the walk under the stars, the song of the pulley, the effort of my arms. It was good for the heart, like a present. When I was a little boy, the lights of the Christmas tree, the music of the Midnight Mass, the tenderness of smiling faces, used to make up, so, the radiance of the gifts I received.

"The people where you live," said the little prince, "raise five thousand roses in the same garden-and they do not find in it what they are looking for."

"They do not find it," I replied.

"And yet what they are looking for could be found in one single rose, or in a little water."

"Yes, that is true," I said. And the little prince added:

"But the eyes are blind. One must look with the heart..."

I had drunk the water. I breathed easily. At sunrise the sand is the colour of honey. And that honey colour was making me happy, too. What brought me, then, this sense of grief?

"You must keep your promise," said the little prince, softly, as he sat down beside me once more.

"What promise?"

"You know-a muzzle for my sheep... I am responsible for this flower..."

I took my rough drafts of drawings out of my pocket. The little prince looked them over, and laughed as he said:

"Your baobabs-they look a little like cabbages."

"Oh!"

I had been so proud of my baobabs!

"Your fox-her ears look a little like horns; and they are too long."

And he laughed again.

"You are not fair, little prince," I said. "I don't know how to draw anything except boa constrictors from the outside and boa constrictors from the inside."

"Oh, that will be all right," he said, "children understand."

So then I made a pencil sketch of a muzzle. And as I gave it to him my heart was torn.

"You have plans that I do not know about," I said.

But he did not answer me. He said to me, instead:

"You know-my descent on the earth... Tomorrow will be its anniversary."

Then, after a silence, he went on:

"I came down very near here."

And he flushed.

And once again, without understanding why, I had a queer sense of sorrow. One question, however, occurred to me:

"Then it was not by chance that on the morning when I first met you -a week ago- you were strolling along like that, all alone, a thousand miles from any inhabited region? You were on your way back to the place where you landed?"

The little prince flushed again.

And I added, with some hesitancy:

"Perhaps, it was because of the anniversary?"

The little prince flushed once more. He never answered questions-but when ones flushes does that not mean "Yes"?

"Ah," I said to him, "I am a little frightened-" But he interrupted me.

"Now you must work. You must return to your engine. I

will be waiting for you here. Come back tomorrow evening..."

But I was not reassured. I remembered the fox. One runs the risk of weeping a little, if one lets himself be tamed...

26

Beside the well there was the ruin of an old stone wall. When I came back from my work, the next evening, I saw from some distance away my little prince sitting on top of this wall, with his feet dangling. And I heard him say:

"Then you don't remember. This is not the exact spot."

Another voice must have answered him, for he replied to it:

"Yes, yes! It is the right day, but this is not the place."

I continued my walk toward the wall. At no time did I see or hear anyone. The little prince, however, replied once again:

"-Exactly. You will see where my track begins, in the sand. You have nothing to do but wait for me there. I shall be there tonight."

I was only twenty yards from the wall, and I still saw nothing.

After a silence the little prince spoke again:

"You have good poison? You are sure that it will not make me suffer too long?"

I stopped in my tracks, my heart torn asunder; but still I did not understand.

Now go away," said the little prince. "I want to get down from the wall."

I dropped my eyes, then, to the foot of the wall-and I leaped into the air. There before me, facing the little prince, was one of those yellow snakes that take thirty seconds to bring your life to an end. Even as I was digging into my pocket to get out my revolver I made a running step back. But, at the noise I made, the snake let himself flow easily across the sand like the dying spray of a fountain, and, in no apparent hurry, disappeared, with a light metallic sound, among the stones.

I reached the wall just in time to catch my little man in my arms; his face was white as snow.

"What does this mean?" I demanded. "Why are you talking with snakes?"

I had loosened the golden muffler that he always wore. I had moistened his temples, and had given him some water to drink.

 THE LITTLE PRINCE

And now I did not dare ask him any more questions. He looked at me very gravely, and put his arms around my neck. I felt his heart beating like the heart of a dying bird, shot with someone's rifle...

"I am glad that you have found what was the matter with your engine," he said. "Now you can go back home-"

"How do you know about that?"

I was just coming to tell him that my work had been successful, beyond anything that I had dared to hope.

He made no answer to my question, but he added:

"I, too, am going back home today..."

Then, sadly-

"It is much farther... It is much more difficult..."

I realized clearly that something extraordinary was happening. I was holding him close in my arms as if he were a little child; and yet it seemed to me that he was rushing headlong toward an abyss from which I could do nothing to restrain him...

His look was very serious, like some one lost far away.

"I have your sheep. And I have the sheep's box. And I have the muzzle..."

And he gave me a sad smile.

I waited for a long time. I could see that he was reviving little by little.

"Dear little man," I said to him, "You are afraid…"

He was afraid, there was no doubt about that. But he laughed lightly.

"I shall be much more afraid this evening…"

Once again I felt myself frozen by the sense of something irreparable. And I knew that I could not bear the thought of never hearing that laughter any more. For me, it was like a spring of fresh water in the desert.

"Little man," I said, "I want to hear you laugh again."

But he said to me:

"Tonight, it will be a year… My star, then, can be found right above the place where I came to the Earth, a year ago…"

"Little man," I said, "tell me that it is only a bad dream- this affair of the snake, and the meeting-place, and the star…"

But he did not answer my plea. He said to me, instead: "The thing that is important is the thing that is not seen…"

"Yes, I know…"

"It is just as it is with the flower. If you love a flower that lives on a star, it is sweet to look at the sky at night. All the stars are a-bloom with flowers…"

"Yes, I know…"

"It is just as it is with the water. Because of the pulley, and the rope, what you gave me to drink was like music. You remember- how good it was."

"Yes, I know…"

"And at night you will look up at the stars. Where I live everything is so small that I cannot show you where my star is to be found. It is better, like that. My star will be just one of the stars, for you. And so you will love to watch all the stars in the heavens... They will all be your friends. And, besides, I am going to make you a present..."

He laughed again.

"Ah, little prince, dear little prince! I love to hear that laughter!"

"That is my present. Just that. It will be as it was when we drank the water..."

"What are you trying to say?"

"All people have stars," he answered, "but they are not the same things for different people. For some, who are travellers, the stars are guides. For others they are no more than little lights in the sky. For others, who are scholars, they are problems. For my businessman they are wealth. But all these stars are silent. You -you alone- will have the stars as no one else has them-"

"What are you trying to say?"

"In one of the stars I shall be living. In one of them I shall be laughing. And so it will be as if all the stars were laughing, when you look at the sky at night... You -only you- will have stars than can laugh!"

And he laughed again.

"And when your sorrow is comforted (time soothes all sorrows) you will be content that you have known me. You will always be my friend. You will want to laugh with me. And you will sometimes open your window, so, for that pleasure... And your friends will be properly astonished to see you laughing as you look up at the sky! Then you will say to them, 'Yes, the stars always make me laugh!' And they will think you are crazy. It will be a very shabby trick that I shall have played on you... "

And he laughed again.

"It will be as if, in place of the stars, I had given you a great number of little bells that knew how to laugh…"

And he laughed again. Then he quickly became serious:

"Tonight – you know… Do not come."

"I shall not leave you," I said.

"I shall look as if I were suffering. I shall look a little as if I were dying. It is like that. Do not come to see that. It is not worth the trouble…"

"I shall not leave you."

But he was worried.

"I tell you-it is also because of the snake. He must not bite you. Snakes-they are malicious creatures. This one might bite you just for fun…"

"I shall not leave you."

But a thought came to reassure him:

"It is true that they have no more poison for a second bite."

That might I did not see him set out on his way. He got away from me without making a sound. When I succeeded in catching up with him he was walking along with a quick and resolute step. He said to me merely:

"Ah! You are there…"

And he took me by the hand. But he was still worrying. "It was wrong of you to come. You will suffer. I shall look as if I were dead; and that will not be true…

" I said nothing.

"You understand… It is too far. I cannot carry this body with me. It is too heavy."

I said nothing.

"But it will be like an old abandoned shell. There is nothing sad about old shells..."

I said nothing.

He was a little discouraged. But he made one more effort:

"You know, it will be very nice. I, too, shall look at the stars. All the stars will be wells with a rusty pulley. All the stars will pour out fresh water for me to drink..."

I said nothing.

"That will be so amusing! You will have five hundred million little bells, and I shall have five hundred million springs of fresh water..."

And he too said nothing more, because he was crying... "Here it is. Let me go on by myself."

And he sat down, because he was afraid. Then he said, again:

"You know-my flower... I am responsible for her. And she is so weak! She is so naïve! She has four thorns, of no use at all, to protect herself against the world..."

I too sat down, because I was not able to stand up any longer.

"There now-that is all..."

He still hesitated a little; then he got up. He took one step. I could not move.

There was nothing there but a flash of yellow close to his ankle. He remained motionless for an instant He did not cry out He feel as gently as a tree falls There was not even any sound, because of the sand.

27

And now six years have already gone by... I have never yet told this story. The companions who met me on my return were well content to see me alive. I was sad, but I told them: "I am tired."

Now my sorrow is comforted a little. That is to say- not entirely. But I know that he did go back to his planet, because I did not find his body at daybreak. It was not such a heavy body... And at night I love to listen to the stars. It is like five hundred million little bells...

But there is one extraordinary thing... When I drew the muzzle for the little prince, I forgot to add the leather strap to it. He will never have been able to fasten it on his sheep. So now I keep wondering: what is happening on his planet? Perhaps the sheep has eaten the flower...

At one time I say to myself: "Surely not! The little prince shuts his flower under her glass globe every night, and he watches over his sheep very carefully..." Then I am happy. And there is sweetness in the laughter of all stars.

But at another time I say to myself: "At some moment or other one is absent-minded, and that is enough! On some one evening he forgot the glass globe, or the sheep got out, without making any noise, in the night…" And then the little bells are changed to tears…

Here, then, is a great mystery. For you who also love the little prince, and for me, nothing in the universe can be the same if somewhere, we do not know where, a sheep that we never saw -yes or no?- eaten a rose…

Look up at the sky. Ask yourselves: Is it yes or no? Has the sheep eaten the flower? And you will see how everything changes

And no grown-up will understand that this is a matter of so much importance!

This is, to me, the loveliest and saddest landscape in the world. It is the same as that on the page before, but I have drawn it again to impress it on your memory. It is here that the little prince appeared on Earth, and disappeared.

Look at it carefully so that you will be sure to recognize it in case you travel some day to the African desert. And, if you should come upon this spot, please do not hurry on. Wait for a time, exactly under the star. Then, if a little man appears who laughs, who has golden hair and who refuses to answer questions, you will know who he is. If this should happen, please comfort me. Send me word that he has come back.